LEGO CITY

WORK THIS FARM!

By Michael Anthony Steele

Illustrated by Chuck Primeau

SCHOLASTIC INC.

NEW YORK   TORONTO   LONDON   AUCKLAND

SYDNEY   MEXICO CITY   NEW DELHI   HONG KONG

ISBN 978-0-545-29857-5

19 18 17 16   14 15/0

Printed in the U.S.A.   40
This edition first printing, March 2011

A farm is a place where farmers raise animals and grow plants. A lot of the food people eat comes from farms. Running a farm takes a lot of work!

First the farmers milk the cows. The big animals are in their stalls, ready and waiting.

Moooooo!

The cows eat hay for breakfast while the farmers get the milk. Hay is a special kind of grass that many farm animals eat.

Pigs eat hay, too. But they eat almost anything! The farmer gives the pigs fresh water to drink. Pigs also like water squirted into their pen to make mud. There's nothing a pig likes more than rolling around in cool mud on a hot day!

Now it's time to exercise the horses. The horses work hard just like the farmers. The horses stay in shape by running and jumping.

A new horse has arrived! The horse is sure to like his new home on the farm.

"Let's see," says the farmer. "With another mouth to feed, I'd better get more hay!"

The farmer gets more hay from the top of the barn. The barn keeps the hay nice and dry.

The hay has to stay clean and fresh so it can be fed to the animals all year long.

A big farm needs big machines! Tractors use their big wheels and strong engines to do all kinds of jobs. They plow fields, pull trailers, and haul heavy loads.

RUMMMMMMMMBLE!
The farmer rides out to the fields. He checks to see if the carrots are ready to be picked.

"These carrots aren't ready yet," says the farmer. "But I know the wheat is ready!" It's time for a really big farm machine!

SWOOSH-SWOOSH-SWOOSH!
Here comes the combine harvester! This machine rolls across the field cutting the tall wheat.

Wheat is a plant that is used to make flour.
Flour is used to make all kinds of foods such
as bread, pasta, and cakes.

This machine is called a "combine" because it combines the jobs of cutting the wheat grass and separating the tiny wheat seeds. The seeds, or grain, are then poured into a trailer nearby.

Later the grain is stored in a silo to keep it dry and safe. While the wheat is loaded into the silo, a delivery truck is filled with fresh vegetables. Soon, these tasty treats will be in markets all over LEGO® City!

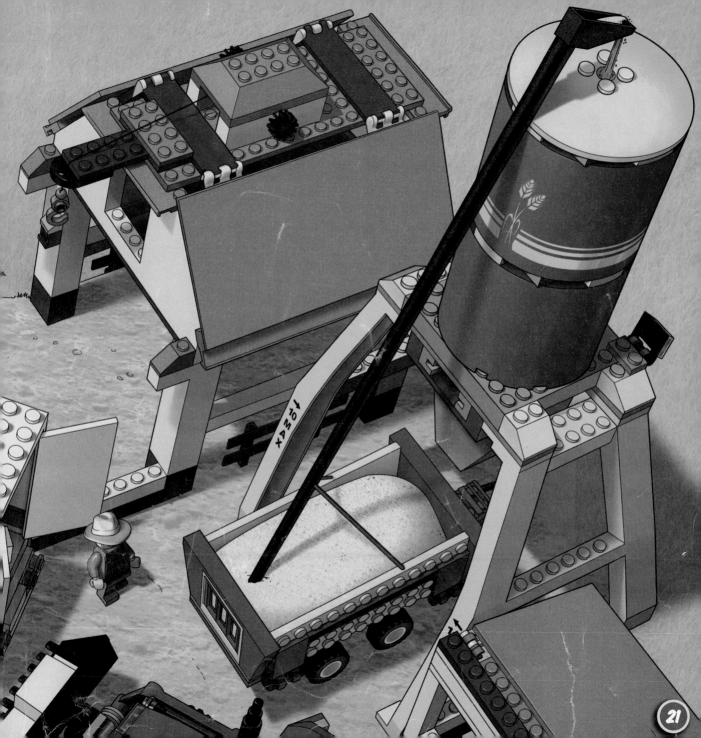

With the vegetables on their way to the city, it's time for dinner!

There are plenty of healthy vegetables from the fields. There is warm bread made from the wheat. And a cool glass of milk to wash it all down.

"Great job, everyone," says the farmer. "Now let's eat!"

Big trucks work in the city—and on the farm!